BEAR AT WORK

Written by Stella Blackstone
Illustrated by Debbie Harter

POST OFFICE

Barefoot Books
Step inside a story

Bear at work is as busy as can be,
Bringing lots of surprises to you
and to me.

He has postcards for the florist
and letters for the baker.

He has cartons for the corner shop
that sells the morning papers.

He strides past every house and home,
stopping here and there.

He brings books to the librarian across the market square.

He steps inside the café,
where he has a cup of tea.

At the school, he gives a package to the children in Room Three.

He has letters for the farmer,
who has recently been wed.

He even has a present for
the little bear in bed.

At last his sack is empty.
Bear's working day is done.
He'll be out again tomorrow,
working hard and having fun!

Bears at Work

Can you spot these working bears in the story?
What would you like to do when you grow up?

florist

baker

shopkeeper

builder

librarian

waitress

teacher

farmer

doctor

postman

For more fun with Bear:

BEAR IN A SQUARE
Stella Blackstone
Debbie Harter

BEAR ON A BIKE
Stella Blackstone
Debbie Harter

BEAR'S BUSY FAMILY
Stella Blackstone
Debbie Harter

BEAR ABOUT TOWN
Stella Blackstone
Debbie Harter

BEAR IN SUNSHINE
Stella Blackstone
Debbie Harter

BEAR AT HOME
Stella Blackstone
Debbie Harter

BEAR TAKES A TRIP
Stella Blackstone
Debbie Harter

BEAR'S BIRTHDAY
Stella Blackstone
Debbie Harter

**For Jemima, with lots of love — S. B.
For Julia, Isabella and Maurice — D. H.**

Barefoot Books, 294 Banbury Road, Oxford, OX2 7ED
Barefoot Books, 2067 Massachusetts Ave, Cambridge, MA 02140

First published in Great Britain by Barefoot Books, Ltd
and in the United States of America by Barefoot Books, Inc in 2008
All rights reserved

Graphic design by Barefoot Books, Oxford
Reproduction by Grafiscan, Verona
Printed in China on 100% acid-free paper

This book was typeset in Slappy and Futura
The illustrations were prepared in paint,
pen and ink, and crayon

Paperback ISBN 978-1-84686-110-9
Boardbook ISBN 978-1-84686-006-5

British Cataloguing-in-Publication Data:
a catalogue record for this book is available from the British Library
Library of Congress Cataloging-in-Publication Data
under LCCN 2007025059